W9-BVR-951

For Eva Cross —L.G.

For the owls in my life, who encourage me to jump . . . and then fly —R.D.

Text copyright © 2016 by Laura Godwin
Jacket and interior illustrations copyright © 2016 by Rob Dunlavey
All rights reserved.
Published in the United States by
Schwartz & Wade Books,
an imprint of Random House Children's Books,
a division of Penguin Random House LLC, New York.

Schwartz & Wade Books and the colophon are
trademarks of Penguin Random House LLC.

Visit us on the Web! randomhousekids.com

Educators and librarians, for a variety of teaching tools,
visit us at RHTeachersLibrarians.com

Library of Congress Cataloging-in-Publication Data
Names: Godwin, Laura, author. | Dunlavey, Rob, illustrator.
Title: Owl sees owl / by Laura Godwin ; illustrated by Rob Dunlavey.
Description: First Edition. | New York : Schwartz & Wade Books,
[2016] |
Summary: A baby owl leaves the nest one night,
explores the world around him, sees his own reflection,
and then returns to the safety of home.
Identifiers: LCCN 2015036751 | ISBN 978-0-553-49782-3 (hardback) |
ISBN 978-0-553-49783-0 (glb) | ISBN 978-0-553-49784-7 (ebk)
Subjects: | CYAC: Owls—Fiction. | BISAC: JUVENILE FICTION /
Animals / Birds. | JUVENILE FICTION / Animals / General. |
JUVENILE FICTION / Nature & the Natural World / General
(see also headings under Animals).
Classification: LCC PZ7.G5438 Ow 2016 | DDC [E]—dc23

The text of this book is set in Belen.

The illustrations were rendered in watercolor,
colored pencil, ink, collage, and digital media.

Book design by Rachael Cole

MANUFACTURED IN CHINA
2 4 6 8 10 9 7 5 3 1
First Edition

Owl Sees Owl

laura godwin & rob dunlavey

schwartz & wade books · new york

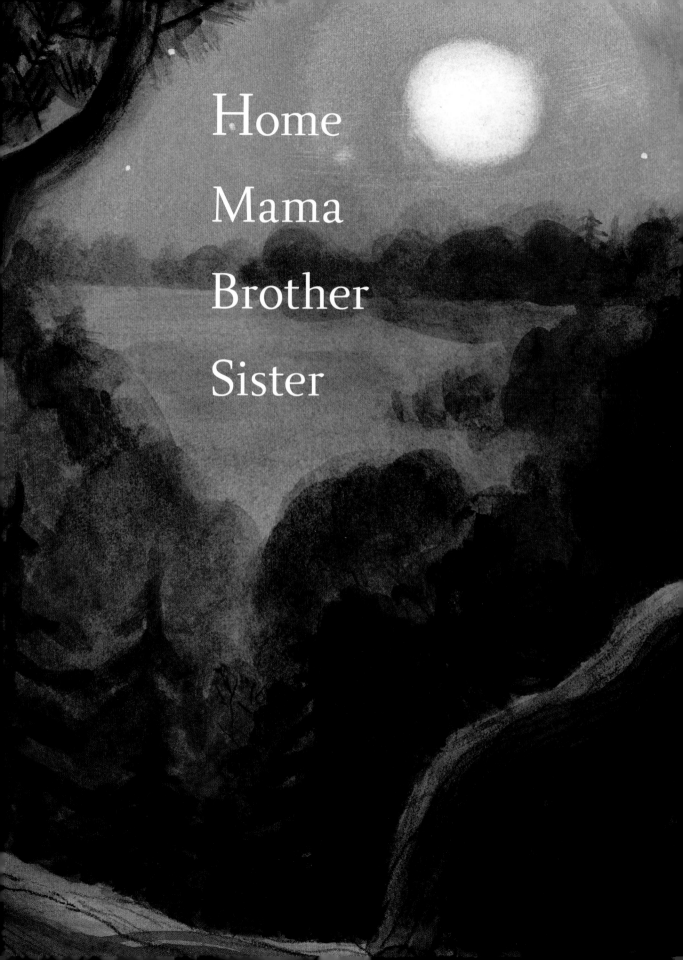

Home
Mama
Brother
Sister

Tree

Nest

Hop

Look

Jump

Flutter

Flap

Fly

Fall
Leaves
Red
Yellow

Moon

Beam

Eyes

Gleam

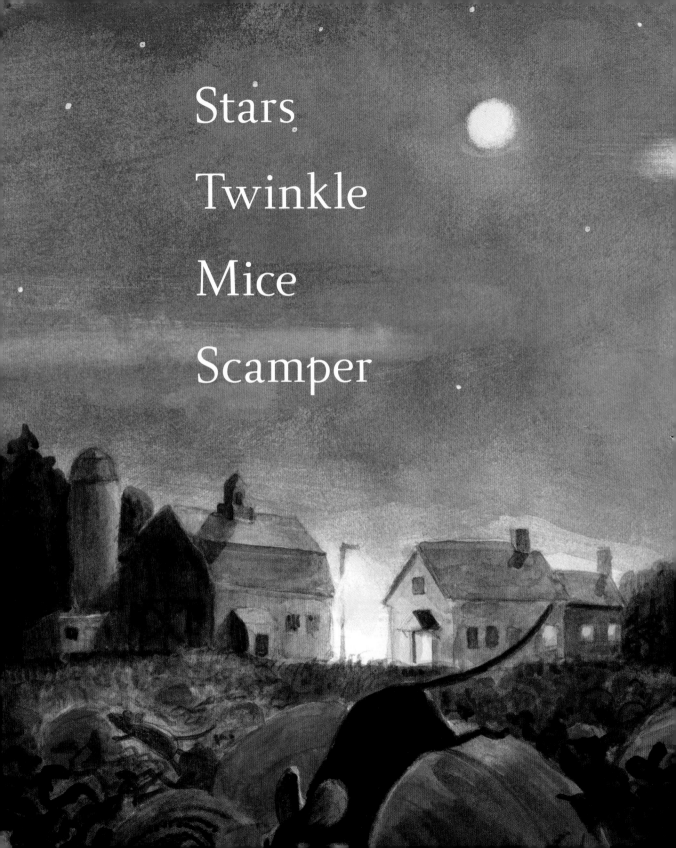

Stars

Twinkle

Mice

Scamper

Soar

Glide

Swoop

Swoosh

Owl

Sees
Owl

Swoosh

Swoop

Glide

Soar

Scamper

Mice

Twinkle

Stars

Gleam

Eyes

Beam

Moon

Yellow

Red

Leaves

Fall

Fly

Flap

Flutter

Jump

Look

Hop

Nest

Tree

Sister

Brother

Mama

Home